هانْسِلْ وغريتِلْ

Hansel and Gretel

Retold by Manju Gregory
Illustrated by Jago

Arabic translation by Wafa' Tarnowska

كانَ يا ما كانَ في قديمِ الزمانِ، حطّابٌ فقيرٌ يَعيشُ معَ زَوْجتِه وَوَلَدَيْهِ في الغابَة.

كانَ اسمُ الصَّبِيِّ هانْسِلْ، واسمُ أُخْتِهِ غريتِلْ. في ذَلِكَ الوَقْتِ، حَلَّتْ علَى الأرْضِ مَجاعَةٌ كَبيرةٌ وَعَظيمَةٌ.

في لَيْلَةٍ من اللَيالي، تَنَهّدَ الأبُ طَويلاً ثُمَّ قالَ لِزَوجتِه: " لا يوجَدُ عِندَنا خُبزٌ كافٍ لِنأكُلَ ".

" اسْمَعْ! " قالَتِ الزَوْجَةُ: " سنَأخُذُ الأوْلادَ إلى الغابَةِ ونَتْرُكُهُما هُناك. هما يَستطيعانِ الاهْتِمامَ بِنَفْسَيهِما ".

فَصَرَخَ الأبُ قائِلاً: " لَكِنَّ الوُحوشَ البَرِّيَّةَ ستُمَزِّقُهُما قِطَعاً قِطَعاً! "

فَرَدَّتْ: " هَلْ تُريدُنا أنْ نموتَ جَميعاً؟ " وَظَلَّتِ الزَوْجَةُ تُجادِلُ زَوجَها حَتّى قَبِلَ بِرَأيِها.

Once upon a time, long ago, there lived a poor woodcutter with his wife and two children. The boy's name was Hansel and his sister's, Gretel. At this time a great and terrible famine had spread throughout the land. One evening the father turned to his wife and sighed, "There is scarcely enough bread to feed us."

"Listen to me," said his wife. "We will take the children into the wood and leave them there. They can take care of themselves."

"But they could be torn apart by wild beasts!" he cried.
"Do you want us all to die?" she said. And the man's wife went on and on and on, until he agreed.

لَمْ يكُنِ الوَلَدانِ نائِمَيْنِ، لأنَّهُما كانا جائِعَيْنِ وقَلِقَيْنِ.

فقَدْ سَمِعا كُلَّ كلِمَةٍ. فبَكَتْ غرِيتْل دُمُوعاً مُرَّةً.

" لا تَقْلَقي، " قالَ هانْسِلْ، " أظُنُّ أنَّني أعْلَمُ كَيفَ يُمْكِنُ أنْ نخَلِّصَ نفُسَينا ".

فخَرجَ إلى الحَديقةِ خِلْسَةً على أطْرافِ أصَابِعِ قَدَمَيه. رَأى في ضَوْءِ القَمَرِ، على الطَريقِ،
بَحْصاً صَغيراً أبْيَضَ يَلْمَعُ كدَراهِمَ فضِّيَةٍ. ملأ هانْسِل جُيُوبَهُ بحَصا ورَجعَ ليُطَمْئِنَ أُخْتَهُ.

The two children lay awake, restless and weak with hunger.
They had heard every word, and Gretel wept bitter tears.
"Don't worry," said Hansel, "I think I know how we can save ourselves."
He tiptoed out into the garden. Under the light of the moon, bright white pebbles shone
like silver coins on the pathway. Hansel filled his pockets with pebbles and returned to
comfort his sister.

باكِراً في الصَّباح التالي، قَبْلَ شُروقِ الشَّمْسِ، أَيْقَظَتِ الأُمُّ هانْسِلْ وغرِيتل بِهَزِّهِما.

" اسْتَيْقِظا، سَنَذْهَبُ إلى الغابَةِ. هذه قِطْعَةُ خُبْزٍ لِكُلٍّ مِنْكُما، لكِنْ لا تَأْكُلاها على الفَوْرِ ".

وخَرَجوا كُلُّهُمْ سَوِيًّا. كان هانْسِلْ يَتَوَقَّفُ مِن حينٍ الى حينٍ وَيَنْظُرُ خَلْفَهُ إلى بَيْتِهِ.

" ماذا تَفْعَلُ؟ " صَرَخَ الأبُ.

" إنَّما أُوَدِّعُ هِرَّتي البَيْضاءَ الجالِسَةَ على السَطْحِ ".

" ما هذا الكلامُ الفارِغُ! " أجَابَتِ الأُمُّ.

" تَكَلَّمِ الحَقِيقَةَ. ها هو ضَوْءُ شَمْسِ الصَّباحِ يَشِعُّ على المَدْخَنَةِ ".

في هذا الوقتِ كانَ هانْسِلْ يَرْمي البَحْصَ الأبيَضَ وَرَاءَهُ على الطَّرِيقِ.

Early next morning, even before sunrise, the mother shook Hansel and Gretel awake.
"Get up, we are going into the wood. Here's a piece of bread for each of you, but don't eat it all at once."
They all set off together. Hansel stopped every now and then and looked back towards his home.
"What are you doing?" shouted his father.
"Only waving goodbye to my little white cat who sits on the roof."
"Rubbish!" replied his mother. "Speak the truth. That is the morning sun shining on the chimney pot."
Secretly Hansel was dropping white pebbles along the pathway.

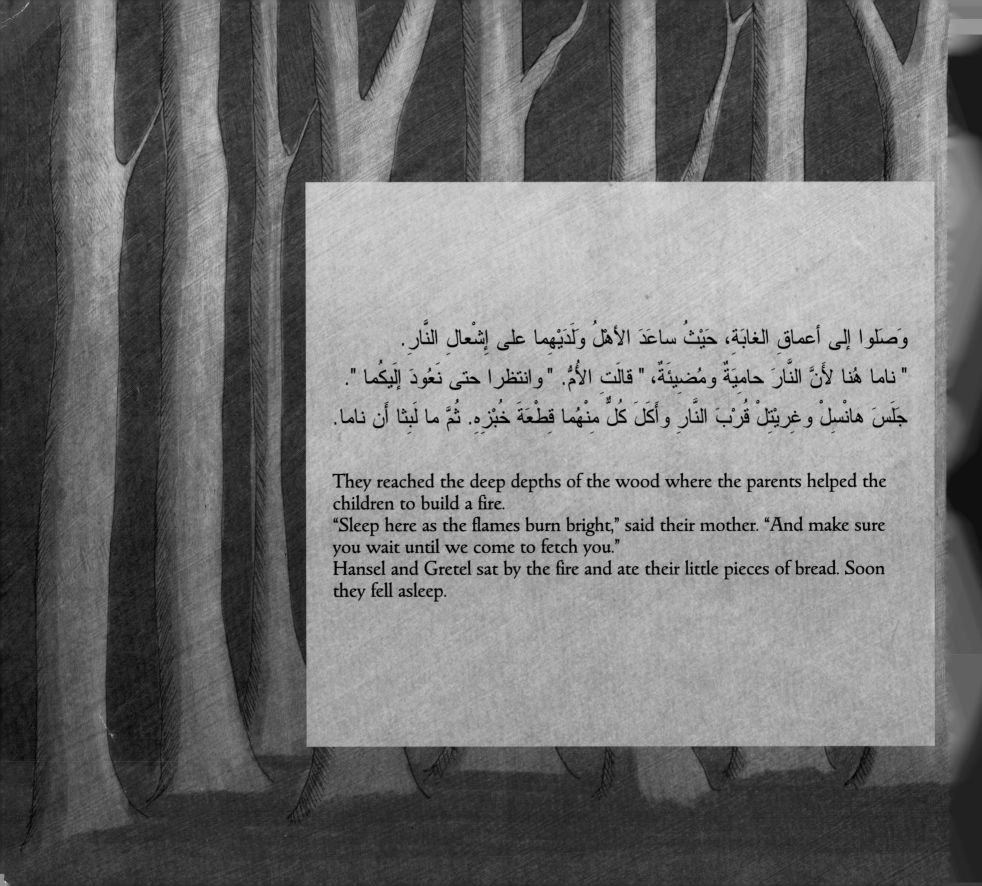

وَصَلوا إلى أعماقِ الغابَة، حَيْثُ ساعَدَ الأهلُ وَلَدَيْهِما على إِشْعالِ النَّارِ.

"ناما هُنا لأَنَّ النَّارَ حامِيَةٌ ومُضيئَةٌ،" قالَتِ الأُمُّ. "وانتظِرا حتى نَعُودَ إِلَيكُما".

جَلَسَ هانْسِلْ وغِريتِلْ قُرْبَ النَّارِ وأَكَلَ كُلٌّ مِنْهُما قِطْعَةَ خُبْزِهِ. ثُمَّ ما لَبِثا أن ناما.

They reached the deep depths of the wood where the parents helped the children to build a fire.

"Sleep here as the flames burn bright," said their mother. "And make sure you wait until we come to fetch you."

Hansel and Gretel sat by the fire and ate their little pieces of bread. Soon they fell asleep.

عِنْدما استَيْقظا كانَتِ الغابَةُ سوداءَ حالِكَةً. صَرَخَتْ غريتِلْ بِبؤْسٍ: " كَيْفَ سَنَرْجِعُ إلى بَيْتِنا؟ "
" انْتَظِري حَتَّى يَطْلَعَ القَمَرُ البَدْرُ، " أَجابَ هانْسِلْ. " عِنْدَها، سَنَسْتَطيعُ رؤْيَةَ البَحْصِ اللّامِعِ ".
انْتَظَرَتْ غريتِلْ حَتَّى تَحَوَّلَ الظلامُ إلى نورٍ. ثمَّ أمْسكَتْ بِيَدِ أخيها وَمَشيا سَوِيًّا واجِدينِ
طَريقَهُما عَلى ضَوْءِ البَحْصِ اللّامِعِ.

When they awoke the woods were pitch black.
Gretel cried miserably, "How will we get home?"
"Just wait until the full moon rises," said Hansel. "Then we will see the shiny pebbles."
Gretel watched the darkness turn to moonlight. She held her brother's hand and together
they walked, finding their way by the light of the glittering pebbles.

في الصَّبَاحِ وَصَلا إلى بَيْتِ أبيهما الحَطَّابِ. عِندَما فَتَحَتِ الأُمُّ البابَ صَرَخَتْ: "لماذا نِمتُما في الغابَةِ طَويلاً؟ ظنَنْتُ أنَّكُما لَنْ تَرْجِعا أبَداً إلى البَيْتِ ".

كانَتِ الأُمُّ مُضْطَربةً. لَكِنَّ أباهُما كانَ سَعيداً إذْ كانَ أكْرَهَ عَلْيهِ أنْ يَتْرُكَهُما وحْدَهُما.

مَرَّتِ الأيَّامُ. وَمَعَ ذلِكَ لَمْ يَكُنْ يُوجَدُ طَعَامٌ كافٍ لإطْعامِ العَائلَةِ.

في لَيْلَةٍ مِنَ اللَيالِي، سَمِعَ هانْسِلْ أُمَّهُ تَقُولُ: "يَجبُ أنْ يذْهَبَ الأولادُ مِنْ هُنا. سَنأْخُذُهُما إلى أبْعَدِ مكانٍ في الغابَةِ. هذه المَرَّةَ لَنْ يَسْتَطيعا أنْ يَجِدا طَريقَ العَوْدَةِ ".

تَسَلَّلَ هانْسِل من سَريرِهِ لِيَجْمَعَ البَحْصَ مَرَّةً أُخْرى. لَكِنْ هذه المَرَّةُ كان البابُ مُغْلَقا.

" لا تَبْكِ، " قالَ لِغرِيتِلْ. " سَأُفَكِّرُ بشيْءٍ ما، اِذْهَبي ونامي الآنَ! "

Towards morning they reached the woodcutter's cottage.
As she opened the door their mother yelled, "Why have you slept so long in the woods?
I thought you were never coming home."
She was furious, but their father was happy. He had hated leaving them all alone.

Time passed. Still there was not enough food to feed the family.
One night Hansel and Gretel overheard their mother saying, "The children must go.
We will take them further into the woods. This time they will not find their way out."
Hansel crept from his bed to collect pebbles again but this time the door was locked.
"Don't cry," he told Gretel. "I will think of something. Go to sleep now."

في اليَوْمِ التَّالي، حَمَلا مَعَهُما لِرِحْلَتِهِما قِطَعَ خُبْزٍ أَصْغَرَ، ثُمَّ أُخِذَ الوَلَدانِ إلى مَكانٍ بَعِيدٍ في الغابَةِ لَمْ يكُن يَعْرفانه أبَداً.

مِنَ حِينٍ إلى حِينٍ كانَ هانْسِلْ يَتَوَقَّفُ ويَرمْي فُتاتَ الخُبْزِ على الأرْضِ.

أشْعَلَ الأهْلُ النارَ وقالا لَهُما أنْ يَناما قُرْبَها. "نَحْنُ ذاهِبانِ لِقَطْعِ الحَطَبِ وسَنَرجِعُ إلَيكُما عِندَما نَنْتَهي مِن عَمَلِنا، " قالَتِ الأُمُّ.

أعْطَتْ غريتِلْ نِصْفَ حِصَّتِها مِن الخُبْزِ لِهانْسِلْ ثُمَّ انْتَظَرا وانْتَظَرا. لكن لَمْ يجِئْ أحَدٌ: قالَ هانْسِلْ: " عِندَما يطْلَعُ القَمَرُ سَيُمكِنُنا أنْ نَرى فُتاتَ الخُبْزِ ونجِدَ طَريقَنا إلى البَيْتَ ".

طَلَعَ القَمَرُ، لكنَّ فُتاتَ الخُبْزِ كانَ قَدْ اخْتَفَى، إذْ أنَّ حَيَواناتِ الغابةِ وعَصافيرَها كانت قَدْ أكَلَتها كُلَّها.

The next day, with even smaller pieces of bread for their journey, the children were led to a place deep in the woods where they had never been before. Every now and then Hansel stopped and threw crumbs onto the ground.
Their parents lit a fire and told them to sleep. "We are going to cut wood, and will fetch you when the work is done," said their mother.
Gretel shared her bread with Hansel and they both waited and waited. But no one came.
"When the moon rises we'll see the crumbs of bread and find our way home," said Hansel.
The moon rose but the crumbs were gone.
The birds and animals of the
wood had eaten every one.

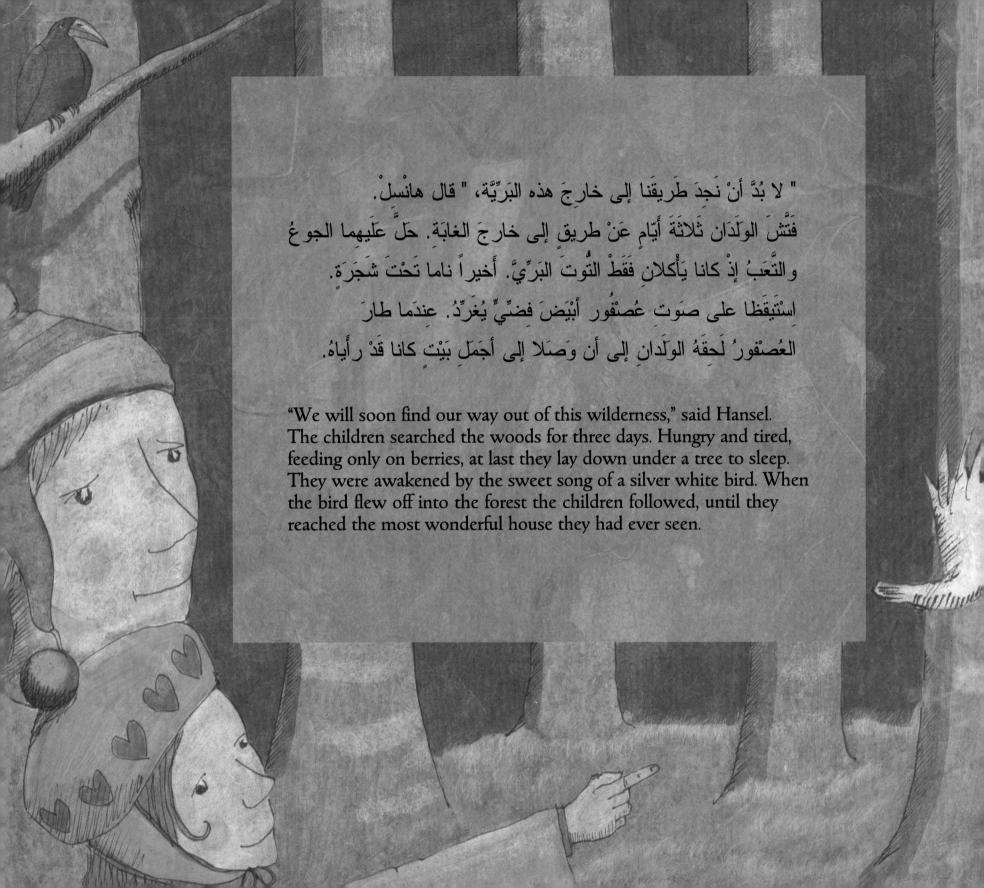

" لا بُدَّ أنْ نَجِدَ طَريقَنا إلى خارِجَ هذه البَرِّيَّة، " قال هانْسِلْ.
فَتَّشَ الوَلَدَان ثَلاثَةَ أَيَّامٍ عَنْ طريقٍ إلى خارِجَ الغابَة. حَلَّ عَلَيهِما الجوعُ
والتَّعَبُ إذْ كانا يَأْكلانِ فَقَطْ التُّوتَ البَرِّيَّ. أخيراً ناما تَحْتَ شَجَرَة.
اسْتَيقَظا على صَوتِ عُصْفُورٍ أبْيَضَ فِضِّيٍّ يُغَرِّدُ. عِندَما طارَ
العُصفُورُ لَحِقَهُ الوَلَدَانِ إلى أن وَصَلا إلى أجْمَلِ بَيْتٍ كانا قَدْ رأياهُ.

"We will soon find our way out of this wilderness," said Hansel.
The children searched the woods for three days. Hungry and tired,
feeding only on berries, at last they lay down under a tree to sleep.
They were awakened by the sweet song of a silver white bird. When
the bird flew off into the forest the children followed, until they
reached the most wonderful house they had ever seen.

The walls were tiled with strawberry tarts, the roof was made of chocolate hearts. Around the windows were caramel frames and the pathway was lined with candy canes. "Now we can eat!" said Hansel and he bit off a piece of the roof.

Suddenly, they heard a voice. "Jimney, Jimney, who's that nibbling at my chimney?"

"It's the wind, it blows right in," they answered, and went on eating.

All at once the door opened and a strange, shrivelled woman appeared. Beyond her tiny spectacles she had blood red eyes.

Hansel and Gretel were so frightened they dropped their sweets.

"What brought you here, my dears?" she said. "If it is hunger, then come and see what I have for you."

She took them by the hand and led them into her little house.

كَانَتْ جُدْرانُهُ مُبَلَّطَةً بِحَلْوَى الفَراوِلَةِ، وكانَتْ أُطُرُ شَبَابِيكِهِ مِن حَلْوى السُّكَّرِ المَحْروقِ، وكانَتِ الطريقُ المُؤَدِّيَةُ إلي البيتِ مُزَيَّنَةً بِسَكاكِرَ على شَكْلِ قَصَبٍ.

" الآنَ يُمكِنُنا أنْ نأكُلَ! " قالَ هانْسِلِ. فأَخَذَ قِطعةً من السَّقْفِ وقَرَشَها.

فَجأةً سَمِعَ صَوْتاً يقولُ: " جَدحْنَتِي جَدحْنَتِي مَنْ يَأْكُلُ من مَدْخَنَتِي؟ "

" هذا الهواءُ يُصَفِّرُ داخِلَها، " أجابَ الوَلَدان وَتابَعا الأَكْلَ.

فَجْأةً فُتِحَ البابُ وأَطَلَّت امْرأةٌ عَجوزٌ غَريبةٌ مُجَعَّدَةٌ. كانَتْ عَيْناها مِن وراءِ نَظارَتَيْها حَمْراوَيْنِ مِثلَ الدَّمِ.

رُعِبَ هَانْسِلِ وغريتِلْ رعبا شديداً فأوْقَعا السَّكاكِرَ مِن أيْدِيهِما.

" ما الذي جَلَبَكُما إلى هُنا يا حبيبي؟ " سَألَتِ العَجوزُ.

" إذا كانَ الجُوعُ، فتَعَالا لِرُؤيَةِ ما عِندي لَكُما ".

فَأَخَذَتهُما بِأيْدِيهِما وأدْخَلَتْهُما إلى بَيْتِها الصَّغِيرِ.

في الصَّبَاحِ أخَذَتِ السَّاحِرةُ الشِّرِّيرةُ هَانْسِل ودَفَعَتْهُ في قفَصٍ وأغْلَقَتْ عَلَيْهِ البابَ.

ارْتَعَبَ هَانْسِل وَصَرَخَ طالِباً النَّجْدَةَ.

أسرَعَتْ غريتِل راكِضةً وصَاحَتْ: " ماذا تَفْعَلينَ بأخي؟ "

ضحِكتِ السَّاحِرةُ ورَفَعَتْ عَيْنَيْهَا الحَمْرَاوَيْنَ مِثْلَ الدَّمِ وأجابَتْ: " إنَّني اسْتَعِدُّ لآكْلِهِ. وأنتِ يا ابْنَتي الصَغيرة، ستُساعِدينَني ". ارتَعَبَتْ غريتِل.

ثمَّ دَفَعَتْها السَّاحِرةُ إلى المَطْبَخِ حَيْثُ أمَرَتْها بتَحضيرِ كَمِّياتٍ كبيرةٍ مِنَ الطَّعَامِ لأخيها.

لَكِنَّ أخَاها رَفَضَ أن يأكُلَ الاكلَ لِكَي لا يَسْمَنَ.

Hansel and Gretel were given all good things to eat! Apples and nuts, milk, and pancakes covered in honey.
Afterwards they lay down in two little beds covered with white linen and slept as though they were in heaven.
Peering closely at them, the woman said, 'You're both so thin. Dream sweet dreams for now, for tomorrow your nightmares will begin!'
The strange woman with an edible house and poor eyesight had only pretended to be friendly.
Really, she was a wicked witch!

في الصَّباحِ أخذَتِ الساحَرَةُ الشِّرِّيرَةُ هَانسِلْ ودَفَعَتْهُ في قَفَصٍ وأغْلَقَتْ عَلَيهِ البابَ.

ارْتَعَبَ هَانسِلْ وصَرَخَ طالباً النَّجْدَةَ.

أسرَعَتْ غريتِلْ راكِضةً وصاحَتْ: " ماذا تَفْعَلينَ بِأخي؟ "

ضحِكَتِ السّاحِرةُ ورَفَعَتْ عَيْنَيْهَا الحَمْراوَيْنَ مِثلَ الدَّمِ وأجابَتْ: " إنَني اَسْتَعِدُّ لآكْلِه. وأنتِ يا ابْنَتي الصَغِيرةَ، ستُساعِدينَني ". ارتَعَبَتْ غرِيتِلْ.

ثمَّ دَفَعَتْها السّاحِرَةُ إلى المَطْبَخِ حَيْثُ أمَرَتْها بِتَحضيرِ كَمِّياتٍ كبيرةٍ مِنَ الطَّعَامِ لأخيها. لَكِنَّ أخَاها رَفَضَ أن يأكُلَ الاكلَ لِكَي لا يَسْمَنَ.

In the morning the evil witch seized Hansel and shoved him
into a cage. Trapped and terrified he screamed for help.
Gretel came running. "What are you doing to my
brother?" she cried.
The witch laughed and rolled her blood red eyes.
"I'm getting him ready to eat," she replied. "And you're
going to help me, young child."
Gretel was horrified.
She was sent to work in the witch's kitchen
where she prepared great helpings of food for
her brother.
But her brother refused to get fat.

كانَتِ الساحِرَةُ تَزُورُ هَانْسِلْ كُلَّ يَومٍ وتَأْمُرُهُ أَنْ يَمُدَّ أُصْبَعَهُ لِكَيّ تَحُسَّهُ:
" مُدَّ إِصْبَعَكَ كَيْ أَرَى كَمْ أَنْتَ سَمينٌ! "

كانَ هَانْسِلْ يَمُدُّ عَظْمَةَ دَجاجٍ كانَتْ في جَيْبِهِ. أمَّا السّاحِرَةُ ذاتُ العَيْنَيْنِ الضَعيفتينِ فَلم تَكُنْ تَفْهَمُ لِمَاذا الصَّبِيُّ ما زالَ نَحيفاً.

بَعْدَ ثَلاثَةِ أسَابِيعَ نَفَذَ صَبَرُها.

قالَتِ الساحِرةُ لغريتِلْ: " اِجْلِبِي الحَطَبَ وأَسْرِعي، يَجِبْ أن نَضعَ هذا الصَّبِيْ في قِدْرِ الطَّبْخِ ".

The witch visited Hansel every day. "Stick out your finger," she snapped. "So I can feel how plump you are!"
Hansel poked out a lucky wishbone he'd kept in his pocket.
The witch, who as you know had very poor eyesight, just couldn't understand why the boy stayed boney thin.
After three weeks she lost her patience.
"Gretel, fetch the wood and hurry up, we're going to get that boy in the cooking pot," said the witch.

حَرَّكَتْ غريتِل نَارَ الفُرْنَ بِبُطْءٍ. كانَتِ الساحِرةُ عَديمَةَ الصَّبْرِ:
" هذا الفُرْنُ يَجبُ أن يَكُونَ قَدْ جَهُزَ الآنَ. اُدْخُلي فيهِ وقُولي لي إذا كانَ حامِياً كافِياً، "
قالَت صارِخة.

فَهِمَتْ غريتِل تَوّاً ما كانَ في بالِ السَّاحِرَةِ. " أنا لا أعْلَمُ كَيفَ؟ " أجابَتْ.
" أنتِ بَلْهاءُ، أنْتِ بنتٌ بَلْهاءُ! " صَرَخَتِ الساحِرةُ بِعُنفٍ. " البابُ مَفْتُوحٌ على مِصْراعَيْهِ،
حَتّى أنا يُمكِنُني أنْ أدْخُلَ فيهِ ".

وَلِإثْباتِ ما كانَتْ تَعْنيهِ أدْخَلَتْ رأْسَها في الفُرنِ جَيِّدًا.
بِسُرْعَةِ البَرقِ دَفَعَتْ غريتْل ما تَبَقَّى من السَّاحِرةِ إلى داخِلِ الفُرْنِ،
وأغْلَقَتِ البابَ عَلَيْها وقَفَلَتْهُ جَيِّدًا. ثم ذَهَبَتْ الى هانْسِل تَصْرُخُ، " ماتَتِ السَّاحِرةُ الشِرِّيرَةُ! "

Gretel slowly stoked the fire for the wood-burning oven.
The witch became impatient. "That oven should be ready by now. Get inside and see if it's hot enough!"
she screamed.
Gretel knew exactly what the witch had in mind. "I don't know how," she said.
"Idiot, you idiot girl!" the witch ranted. "The door is wide enough, even I can get inside!"
And to prove it she stuck her head right in.
Quick as lightning, Gretel pushed the rest of the witch into the burning oven. She shut and bolted the iron
door and ran to Hansel shouting: "The witch is dead! The witch is dead! That's the end of the wicked witch!"

وثَبَ هَانْسِلْ من قَفَصِهِ كَالعُصفُورِ الطائِرِ.

Hansel sprang from the cage like a bird in flight.

عانَقَ هَانْسِلْ وغريتِلْ بَعْضَهُما ثُمَّ رقَصا وغنَّيا وركَضا بِفَرحٍ عَظيمٍ.
في كلِّ زاويَةٍ من البَيْتِ عَثَرا على صنَاديقَ ملآى بالجواهرِ واللؤلؤ
والمُرجانِ والأُرجُوانِ وجَميعِ أنْواعِ الأشْياءِ الثَّمينَةِ.
عَبَّأَ هَانْسِلْ وغريتِلْ جُيُوبَهُما حتى اكْتَظَّتْ.
" لَدَيْنا كُنُوزٌ عَجيبة، لكنْ كَيفَ يُمْكِنُنا أنْ نَهْرُبَ مِنْ هذهِ الغابَةِ الموحِشَةِ؟ "
تَنَهَّدَت غريتِلْ.
" لا تَقْلَقِي، مَعاً سنَعثُرُ على طريقِ العَوْدةِ إلى البَيْتِ، " قالَ هَانْسِلْ.

Hansel and Gretel hugged each other. They danced and sang and ran around with joy. In every corner they found treasure chests filled with pearls, emeralds, rubies and all kinds of worldly precious things. Hansel and Gretel filled their pockets to overflowing.
"We have wondrous treasures, but how do we escape from the wild wood?" sighed Gretel.
"Don't worry, together we will find our way home," said Hansel.

بَعْدَ ثَلاثِ ساعاتٍ وَصَلا إلى بُقْعَةٍ مِنَ الماءِ.

" لا يُمْكِنُنا أنْ نَعْبُرَ، " قال هَانْسِلْ. " لا يوجَدُ مَرْكَبٌ أو جِسْرٌ، ثَمَّةَ مِياهٌ نَقِيَّةٌ زَرْقاءُ ".

" اُنْظُرْ إلى الماءِ! " قالَتْ غريتِل. " هُناكَ بَطَّةٌ بَيْضاءُ تَعُومُ. رُبَّما تُساعِدُنا ".

فَأَخذا بالغِناءِ مَعاً: " أَيَّتُها البَطَّةُ الصَّغيرةُ، ذاتُ الجَوانِحِ البَيْضاءِ، اللاَّمِعَةِ،

اِسْمَعي مِن فَضْلِكِ، المِياهُ عميقةٌ، والمِياهُ واسِعَةٌ، هَلْ يُمْكِنُكِ حَمْلُنا إلى الضِّفَّةِ الأُخْرى؟ "

سَبَحَتِ البَطَّةُ نَحْوَهُما وحَمَلَتْ هَانْسِلْ أَوَّلاً ثُمَّ غريتِل على ظَهْرِها بِسَلامةٍ عَبْرَ الماءِ.

في الضِّفَّةِ الأُخْرى وَجَدَا عالَماً مَألُوفاً.

After three hours they came upon a stretch of water.
"We cannot cross," said Hansel. "There's no boat, no bridge, just clear blue water."
"Look! Over the ripples, a pure white duck is sailing," said Gretel. "Maybe she can help us."
Together they sang: "Little duck whose white wings glisten, please listen.
The water is deep, the water is wide, could you carry us across to the other side?"
The duck swam towards them and carried first Hansel and then Gretel safely across the water.
On the other side they met a familiar world.

خُطْوَةً خُطْوَةً، وجَدا طَريقَهُما إلى مَنْزِلِ الحَطَّابِ.

"رَجَعْنا إلى البَيْتِ!" صَرَخَ الوَلَدانِ.

ابْتَسَمَ الأَبُ ابتِسامَةً عَريضَةً وقال: "لم أُمْضِ دَقيقَةً واحِدةً سَعيدَةً مُنْذُ أن تَرِكْتُما. فَتَّشْتُ عَنْكُما في كُلِّ مكانٍ".

Step by step, they found their way back to the woodcutter's cottage.
"We're home!" the children shouted.
Their father beamed from ear to ear. "I haven't spent one happy moment since you've been gone," he said.
"I searched, everywhere..."

" أَيْنَ أُمُّنا؟ "

" لَقَدْ ذَهَبَتْ! عِنْدَما لَمْ يكُنْ لَدَينا شَيْءٌ لِنَأْكُلَهُ خَرَجَتْ مِنَ البَيتِ قائِلَةً أَنِّي لَنْ

أَراها مِنْ بَعْدُ. لا يُوجَدُ الآنَ إلاّ نَحْنُ الثَّلاثَةُ ".

" وَأَحْجَارُنا الكَرِيمَةُ " قال هَانْسِلْ، واضِعاً يَدَهُ في جَيْبِهِ، مُبْرِزاً لُؤْلُؤَةً بَيْضاءَ مِثْلَ الثَّلْجِ.

فقالَ الأَبُ: " يَبدو أَنَّ جَمِيعَ مَشاكِلِنا قَدْ انْتَهَتْ ".

"And Mother?"
"She's gone! When there was nothing left to eat she stormed out saying I would never see her again. Now there are just the three of us."
"And our precious gems," said Hansel as he slipped a hand into his pocket and produced a snow white pearl.
"Well," said their father, "it seems all our problems are at an end!"